Hey, guys!

OK, everybody. It's me again, Carly! And I'm here to welcome you to another volume in the ultimate history of iCarly. So as everyone knows, iCarly is officially a hit on the Web. But did you know that we've hit the big time in books, too? And I mean *big* . . . like world's fattest man *big* . . . like 10-foot-tall cup of coffee *big*. Let's just say that Sam, Freddie, Spencer, and I got into a book that even Sam can't put down. (Now THAT'S big.) Just turn the page to find out how we did it. (If you've been eating pudding with your hands, just make sure to wipe them first!) How awesome is that? Check out the cool pics, too. Don't worry — it's way more exciting than the Geometry Channel. Promise!

I'd write more (especially with this tangerine marker. Mmm . . .) but Spencer's making burgers. Catch-up again soon! (Ha!)

Don't forget to keep watching iCarly — Bye for now! (P.S. Freddie says to turn the page QUICK because this book goes live in 5 . . . 4 . . . 3 . . . 2 . . .)

People of Earth — don't miss a single **iCarly** book!

iWant a World Record!

NICKELODEON™

iCarly™

iWant a World Record!

Adapted by Laurie McElroy

Part 1: Based on "iWant a World Record," Written by Dan Schneider

Part 2: Based on "iGot Detention," Written by Andrew Hill Newman

Based on the TV series *iCarly*, Created by Dan Schneider

SCHOLASTIC INC.

New York   Toronto   London   Auckland   Sydney
Mexico City   New Delhi   Hong Kong   Buenos Aires

ISBN–13: 978-0-545-14256-4
ISBN–10: 0-545-14256-3

Published by Scholastic Inc.
SCHOLASTIC and associated logos are trademarks and/or registered trademarks of Scholastic Inc.

12 11 10 9 8 7 6 5 4 3   9 10 11 12 13 14/0

Printed in the U.S.A.
First printing, May 2009

iWant a World Record!

iWant a World Record

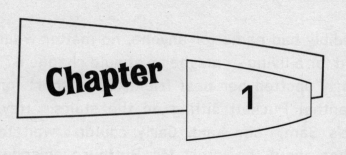

Chapter 1

Carly Shay and her friend Freddie Benson left their Ridgeway School classroom and walked into the hall. The class, led by a substitute teacher, had been a complete disaster. For the teacher anyway. The kids kind of liked it. Spitballs flew, jokes were told, and no one listened to the day's lesson.

"Man, I feel bad. I hate to see a teacher cry like that," Freddie said.

Carly was sympathetic, too. Especially when she saw the substitute teacher practically melt into a puddle of tears, but why didn't the guy do something about it?

"Yeah, but c'mon," Carly told Freddie, "when you're a substitute teacher and your name is Mr. Buttburn, what do you expect?"

"Yeah," Freddie agreed. It was an incredibly bad name for a teacher. Actually, Buttburn was an

3

incredibly bad name for anyone, no matter what he did for a living — maybe he should change it?

Carly spotted her best friend Sam (short for Samantha) Puckett sitting on the stairs. "Hey, there's Sam," she said. Carly couldn't wait to tell her about the latest Mr. Buttburn episode. Sam was positively merciless when it came to tormenting substitute teachers. Actually, Sam was merciless with teachers in general. Carly was forever having to keep her friend from getting into too much trouble.

But Sam wasn't causing any trouble now. She was doing something incredibly unusual. Unusual for Sam that is. She was reading a book!

"What'cha reading?" Carly asked, sitting on the stairs next to Sam.

"The *Jonas Book of World Records*," Sam said, barely looking up from its pages. "This thing's full of top-notch weirdos, mutants, and psychos," she said happily.

"All your favorite things," Carly joked.

"I know!" Sam exclaimed. "Check this out!" She flipped the pages until she came to one of her

favorite records and pointed to the picture. "World's Fattest Man," she read.

Freddie read over her shoulder. "Eight hundred pounds!"

"Holy flab!" Carly laughed. The man was enormous!

"Oh, and this will excite Freddie," Sam said with a sneer. "This year they've got a whole new section for world records in technology." She flipped through the pages again, looking for the right chapter.

Freddie was totally into all things high-tech. Or, as Sam would say, all things high-geek. She was always making fun of him for it. Freddie wasn't as good at snappy comebacks as Sam was. Usually he just got mad and yelled. Carly often found herself playing peacemaker between the two of them.

Freddie tried to play it cool. "Yeah, well guess what? I don't even care about —" It took that long for the words "world records in technology" to sink in. "Give me the book," he said, snatching it from her.

Freddie read the names of some of the technology records out loud, his voice rising with excitement.

"Most Downloaded Image, Fastest Computer Processor."

It was obvious that he found those records totally cool.

"Most boring words ever," Sam mocked.

Freddie ignored her and kept reading. Then he saw something that even Sam couldn't make fun of.

"Hey, hey. Check this out," he said with a note of triumph in his voice. "World's Longest Continuous Webcast."

"Really?" Carly asked, getting to her feet. She took the book from Freddie and read the page. That was a record she could definitely get into.

Carly, Freddie, and Sam had a weekly live Webcast they called *iCarly*. When Carly first got the idea for a Web show, Freddie had immediately volunteered to be the show's technical producer. It helped that he had all the latest camera equipment and knew how to use it. He was always

coming up with new ways to make their show more exciting.

Even the name of the show, *iCarly*, had been Freddie's idea. "i — Internet. Carly — you," he had explained at the time. Carly and Sam both loved it. Ever since, they'd appeared live on their fans' computer screens.

Carly was amazed by how much Freddie knew about that technical stuff. She was glad her job was to be in front of the camera and not behind it. She didn't think she could keep everything running as smoothly as Freddie did.

The show wouldn't run smoothly without Sam either. Sam was Carly's sidekick on the *iCarly* show and in real life. In addition to being a great friend, Sam was crazy, fun, and unpredictable. She was hilarious on and off the Webcast. No one was as good at coming up with wild and crazy ideas as Sam was.

Carly needed both Freddie and Sam to make the show a success, and so far the Webcast had been a hit. More kids were tuning in every week and telling their friends to watch, too. But their audience could always be bigger.

Carly wasn't the only one interested in the world record for the longest continuous Webcast. For once, Sam and Freddie agreed on something — getting a world record would be super-cool.

Sam stood up and looked over Carly's shoulder. "How long?" she asked.

"Twenty-four hours, eight minutes," Carly read.

"Whoa!" Sam said. That was impressive!

"We could beat that," Freddie told them.

"Totally," Carly agreed. "And think about how much buzz *iCarly* would get if we *did* break that record."

Suddenly Sam realized that breaking the record would mean more than just buzz for *iCarly*. "I could get my face in the same book as the world's fattest man," she gasped, totally excited. "Oh my gosh, I would die!"

Their conversation was cut off when the substitute teacher rushed past them with his head down. There was a small crowd of students behind him, all pointing and laughing.

"Mr. Buttburn!" someone yelled.

Everyone howled with laughter.

The teacher was near tears again. "It's not funny!" he insisted. "It's my name."

That didn't stop his students. Carly couldn't exactly blame them. It was a funny name, and so easy to ridicule. Still, hadn't the substitute already been teased enough today?

"Aww," she said. "Poor Mr. Buttburn."

Chapter 2

After school that day, Carly and her friends headed for Carly's apartment to do some serious research into breaking the world record for the longest continuous Webcast. Carly lived in an old high-rise industrial building in downtown Seattle with her twenty-six-year-old brother, Spencer. Spencer was an artist, so when the building was converted to apartments and artists' lofts, they had moved in.

Carly's father, a military officer, was stationed on a submarine. While he was away, Spencer was Carly's guardian. A lot of people thought it was strange that a teenaged girl lived with her twenty-six-year-old brother, but Carly and Spencer wouldn't have it any other way.

Part of the fun of living with an artist was never knowing what new creation Carly would come

home to — a giant robot made out of soda bottles, a fish-feeding machine, a camcorder transformed into a squirrel. Spencer was definitely quirky and offbeat, but he was always there for his little sister. He was totally responsible when it came to the important stuff like making sure Carly ate healthy food and did well in school. Carly helped Spencer tone down some of his wildest ideas. The two of them looked out for each other.

Spencer had been cool with the idea of Carly and her friends turning the third floor of their loft into the *iCarly* studio. It was a big open space, and they had fixed it up so it looked really great. There was plenty of room for all of Freddie's high-tech equipment, and Spencer's light sculptures made awesome props. His sculpture of the front end of a classic car was in the background, along with a wall painted with the moon and stars. There was even a neon *iCarly* Live sign over the window.

But today they were hanging out in the kitchen, not the studio. Carly had done some research on her computer, and now she was on the phone with the world record company.

"Okay, and if we break the world record, we definitely get our picture in the book?" she said into the phone.

Sam interrupted with a question of her own. "Ask her if she knows the fat man."

Carly put her hand over the mouthpiece. "I'm not asking her that," she whispered. Then she spoke into the phone again. "Yeah, I'm still here. Uh-huh."

Freddie looked at the fat man's picture in the book and eyed Sam with a quizzical expression. "Why are you obsessed with fat men?" he asked.

"I'm not," Sam insisted. "I'm obsessed with the *fattest* man. The chubby ones mean nothing to me."

Freddie rolled his eyes. Sam would always be a mystery to him. And quite frankly, he didn't *want* to know what was going on in that brain of hers. The thought was a little scary. He closed the book and handed it to her.

Carly was still speaking to the world record official. "Sure, I'll check all the rules online. Okay. Thanks so much," she said. "Bye."

"What did they say?" Sam asked as soon as Carly hung up.

"That they'll send a person out here to monitor the whole Webcast, and if we go longer than twenty-four hours and eight minutes with no interruptions, *iCarly* will be in the *Jonas Book of World Records*," Carly explained. It sounded pretty simple.

"I cannot wait," Sam said.

"Uh, there's just one problem," Freddie told them.

Sam sighed. "What now?" she asked him.

"What are you guys going to do for twenty-four hours in front of the camera?" he asked.

Carly hadn't thought about that part. Maybe it wasn't so simple after all. "Yeah, what are we going to do?" she asked.

Freddie was ready with a suggestion. In fact it was something he suggested all the time. "Well —"

Carly knew what was coming. She cut him off. "We're not doing 'Tech Time with Freddie,'" she said. She couldn't imagine anything more boring.

"But the *iCarly* viewers would love it," Freddie insisted. "I could talk about dual-density memory chips, the importance of backing up your personal data —"

Now Sam cut him off. "I'd like to back up over your personal data with a truck," she said.

Freddie glared at her. He was trying to come up with a response when they heard a lot of noise coming from the other room. There was a *crash*, followed by a bunch of *clang*s, and then a loud groan from Spencer.

He wheeled a dolly into the living room. It was piled high with plastic bins.

"What'cha doing?" Carly asked.

"I'm trying to find my drill. I think it's in one of these bins," Spencer said. He took the top off of one of the plastic bins and dumped the contents all over the floor. "Help me look," he said.

Carly, Sam, and Freddie got on their knees to help Spencer sort through his stuff.

"Let's see," Carly said, coming across a plastic bat and then a yo-yo.

"Hey!" Spencer yelled, grabbing a small plastic container. "It's my jar of sand from

Mexico." He took the lid off and gave it a big sniff. *"Olé!"*

Sam found a drill in the middle of the pile. "Hey, here's your drill," she said.

Spencer had already forgotten what he was looking for. He was dreaming of Mexican beaches. "Oh yeah, thanks," he said, taking it from her.

Carly looked at the pile of junk in front of her. "Maybe you should get rid of some of this stuff," she suggested.

"I should but I shan't," Spencer told her.

"Is 'shan't' a word?" Carly asked.

"Possibly," Spencer said. "But whether it's 'shan't' or 'shisn't,' I am going to use all this stuff to make a supertastic sculpture that I will call . . ." He paused to think about it for a minute. He didn't have a title. ". . . A Supertastic Sculpture of Stuff," he finally said, waving his arms around grandly.

Carly and her friends just stared at him.

"I know, not a great name for a sculpture," Spencer agreed.

"No, it is shnot," Carly joked.

"Shnot!" Now there's a title, Spencer thought.

A couple of days later, Carly and Sam were dancing around the *iCarly* studio at nine o'clock in the morning, warming up for their record-breaking Webcast while Freddie checked his camera equipment. They needed lots of energy to get through the next twenty-four hours and eight minutes.

Freddie picked up his camera. "All right, girls, let's break a world record," he said. "Ready in five, four, three, two. . . ."

On the number one, the red light on the camera blinked on and Freddie pointed to the girls. That was their signal to start the show.

"Hey, people," Carly said into the camera. "Welcome to *iCarly*!"

"Are you wide awake?" Sam asked.

"You're not?" Carly said.

Carly and Sam both put their faces close to the camera and screamed right into the microphone. They could imagine their viewers jumping back and plugging their ears. "You are now!" they said in unison.

"Which is good," Sam added.

"Because you're going to need to stay awake with us for a *loooooong* time," Carly said.

Sam pretended not to know what was going on. "Why's that, Carly?"

"I think you know, Sam," Carly answered.

Sam grinned and nodded. "Tell me anyway."

As usual, Sam and Carly talked fast and finished each other's sentences.

Carly started to explain. "Because me, Sam, and our technical producer, Freddie, are here to break the record . . ."

". . . for the world's longest live Webcast ever!" Sam finished.

"So we can be in next year's *Jonas Book of World Records*," Carly said, holding up the book.

"And to make it all official . . ." Sam said.

". . . here's an actual representative from the World Record Committee, Marilyn Raymer!" Carly said.

Sam hit a button on the remote control she held in every *iCarly* Webcast. Freddie had created it for her. One button could fill the studio with boos and raspberries, another with sympathetic "aww's," and another with flashing lights and

dance music. The button she pushed now filled the studio with the sound of applause and cheers.

Marilyn Raymer walked into the room and gave the camera a little wave.

"So, Marilyn, go over the rules for our viewers, would you?" Sam asked.

"Well, to beat the world record, your Webcast must be continuous and last longer than twenty-four hours and eight minutes," Marilyn explained. "You can't stop streaming, no breaks, and some-one must be awake and doing something on-screen at all times."

"Awesome," Carly said.

"We got it," Sam added.

"By the way," Marilyn said, "Carly mentioned to me that you might enjoy having this." She unrolled a poster and handed it to Sam.

Sam took the poster and then let out a high-pitched scream. "No way! It's the world's fattest man!" She held the autographed poster up to the camera so that Freddie could get a shot of it. "Look at him!"

"All right, calm down," Carly said. She turned to the camera again and let it follow her as she walked across the room. "Now, over here is our countdown clock."

There was a digital clock hanging on the wall with a sign over it that read "Time Remaining." It was counting down from twenty-four hours and eight minutes to zero. When they reached that, they would tie the record. Then they'd stay on the air an extra minute to make sure they became record breakers. Right now the clock read 24:06. They had been on the air for two minutes.

"It tells us exactly how much time is left until we break the world record," Sam explained.

The clock wasn't the only new thing Carly had to tell the audience about. There was one more addition to their show.

"And just to make sure Sam and I keep up our energy, our tech producer, Freddie, has pre-set a special timer," Carly said.

"We don't know when it's going to go off," Sam said.

"But when it does, you're going to see some —"

Carly's explanation was cut off when Freddie's special timer went off. A loud alarm sounded, followed by the words "Random Dancing" spoken in a deep, loud voice. The lights dimmed and then started to flash. Fun, fast-paced dance music filled the studio.

Carly and Sam both started to dance around like crazy and brought their energy level way up. The clock read 24:04. Only twenty-four hours and four minutes to go!

Chapter 3

Two hours later, the girls were still going strong. They had brought their audience up to date on everything weird and wacky that had happened to them over the past week, told some jokes, and played a few videos that their viewers had sent to the show. Now it was time for a surprise for their viewers.

"Okay! Now we're introducing another new segment," Carly said. "Which we call . . ."

Carly and Sam leaned into the camera. "'Street Fishing!'" they announced in unison.

Freddie hit a button and a "Street Fishing" graphic flashed across the screen.

Carly grabbed a nearby fishing pole. "We're going to cast our line all the way down to the street below and see what we can catch," she said.

Sam opened the window. Carly pulled her arm back and cast the line right out of the window.

"Oh, I forgot my lucky fishing hat," Sam joked. She pulled on a red hat decorated with hooks and lures. Then she put her face directly in front of the camera lens. "Like it?" she asked.

Carly's fishing line looked like it was being pulled from below.

"Hey, hey! I think you got a tug on the line there," Sam said.

"That is a lucky fishing hat!" Carly joked. Something was definitely on the other end of her line.

"Pull it up!" Sam urged.

"I'm pulling!" Carly said. She gave the line one more tug. "Got it!"

Sam reached out to help Carly bring their catch into the studio. Their jaws dropped when they saw what it was. They had caught a baby and yanked it through the window, and now it was crying!

"Oh. My. Gosh!" Sam exclaimed.

Carly's eyes got wide. "We hooked a baby!" she said, sounding totally panicked.

22

"Throw it back!" Sam screamed. Isn't that what you did in fishing when your catch was too small?

"I can't throw it back," Carly said. "It's a baby, and —"

Sam grabbed the baby and turned its face to the camera. It sounded like a real baby's cry, but it was obvious now that it was a doll, not a real baby. Spencer had waited downstairs, and attached the doll to the fishhook when Carly cast her line.

"Just kidding!" the girls said together. They cracked up, imagining how shocked and terrified their viewers must have been.

"It's a fake baby," Carly said.

"See," Sam said, holding the doll even closer to the camera.

Carly reached over and yanked the doll's head off. There was a small popping noise as confetti shot out of the doll's neck, filling the studio with colorful pieces of paper.

Later in the Webcast, Carly and Sam told their viewers about another new segment they had

planned. As usual, Freddie just held the camera steady on both of the girls. They cut back and forth so fast, he never knew who would be speaking next — and sometimes he never knew what they'd say!

"All right, throughout this whole marathon Webcast . . ." Carly started.

Then Sam took over. "Carly's brother, Spencer, is going to stay awake with us . . ."

". . . while he's building an insane new sculpture," Carly explained.

"So let's check in with him," Sam said.

Freddie punched a button on his control panel. "Remote cam up," he said.

The TV monitor on the wall sprang to life, along with a remote camera Freddie had positioned downstairs. It was focused on Spencer and his sculpture.

"Hey, Spencer!" Carly said.

"Yo, Spence!" Sam added.

Spencer ran over to the camera. "Oh, hey, Carly! Sam!"

"So tell us about that sculpture you're making," Carly said.

Spencer pointed to the small pile of junk behind him and to the bigger pile of junk he hadn't yet added to the sculpture, while he described his very big, supertastic plans for the stuff all around him. "Okay! As you can see, it's sort of a mishmash of various parts and items, and when I'm done, a lot of the pieces are going to move around and spin, shake, rattle, roll, and things of that nature."

As he spoke a big object fell off the sculpture with a crash.

"I will fix that," Spencer said.

While Spencer talked, Marilyn Raymer watched the show on her computer screen from a corner in the *iCarly* studio. She had to make sure the show didn't stop streaming even for a second. But she was getting tired of standing around in the loft watching Sam and Carly. She had to keep moving to stay out of the way, and there was no place to sit. She spotted the couch behind Spencer and decided it might be time to watch the show from downstairs.

Carly didn't notice her leave. She was still focused on her brother and his art. "Okay,

Spencer, we'll come back to you in about an hour," she said.

"I will be here!" Spencer told her.

Another piece of his sculpture fell off and landed on the floor with a thud.

"Okay!" Carly said brightly.

Sam was ready to move on, too. She clicked her remote control and turned the monitor off. "And coming up next on *iCarly*," she said, "more wacky videos from our wacky audience."

By then, Marilyn had made her way downstairs with her laptop. "Hi," she said.

Spencer looked up. "Oh, hey there," he said.

"Is it cool if I hang out down here for a while and monitor the Webcast on my laptop?" she asked. "It's a little crowded upstairs."

Spencer smiled. "Oh sure, get yourself comfy," he said, pointing to the couch.

"All right," Marilyn said. "That's a cool sculpture you're working on."

"Ah, thanks. I'm kind of free-forming it, you know?" Spencer said, trying to play it cool. Really he was trying to impress Marilyn. "I just reach into these bins, grab whatever

my hand finds, and *boom* — on the sculpture it goes."

"Fun," Marilyn said.

"Yeah." Spencer stuck his hand into a bin. "I love it because you never know what you're going to find —" He yelped and pulled his hand out of the bin. "Pushpins," he said with a groan showing her his palm. It was covered in at least a dozen multicolored pushpins — Spencer's palm had become a bulletin board!

Marilyn winced. Spencer held his hand out to her so that she could pull out the pushpins, one at a time. He wasn't playing it cool anymore.

"*Ow*, *ow*, *ow*, get them out, get them out!" he said. "The blue one! *Ow!* And the other blue one! *Ow!*" He looked Marilyn in the eyes. "I think we're bonding! *Ow!*"

By six-thirty, Sam and Carly had been on the air for over nine hours, and they were still going strong.

"Okay, as you can see on our fancy countdown clock there . . ." Sam said.

Freddie focused his camera on the clock.

"...we have fourteen hours and thirty-nine minutes left until we break the world record," Carly said.

"So what are we going to do next, Carly?" Sam asked.

"Well, we could —"

Freddie cleared his throat very loudly to get their attention.

"What?" Carly asked.

"What, Freddie?" Sam asked.

But they didn't really have to ask. They knew what Freddie wanted.

"C'mon, let me do it," Freddie pleaded. He was all ready to go. He knew they'd have to break down and say yes at some point during the Webcast.

The girls exchanged looks and rolled their eyes. It was time to give up and let Freddie have his boring segment. He was obviously never going to stop asking.

"Fine," Carly agreed with a sigh. "You can do it."

Freddie was totally excited. He put down his handheld camera and pushed a button on his

control panel before running in front of a station-ary camera, ready and perched on a tripod.

He waved at the camera. "Hey, people. I'm Freddie Benson, the technical producer of *iCarly*. And this is a new segment I like to call..." He stopped and ran over to his control panel to press a button, and then back in front of the cam-era. A graphic that read "Tech Time with Freddie" appeared on the viewers' computer screens just as Freddie said the words.

Sam pushed the button on her remote that filled the studio with boos and raspberries.

Carly wasn't any more enthusiastic, but she tried to play along. "So, Freddie, what fun techno-logical thing do you have to show us?" she asked with a fake smile.

Freddie didn't notice her lack of enthusiasm. Or he didn't care. He was just excited to share his love of all things technical with their audience — *finally*. "I'm glad you asked, Carly. I'm going to show you guys this new high-tech lightbulb."

Sam stood behind Freddie, making faces and rolling her eyes. She was sure that their viewers

would be bored to death by Freddie's geeky segment and wanted to give them something more interesting to watch.

Freddie didn't notice her. He waved what looked like a normal, compact florescent lightbulb in front of the camera. But this one was different. "It's filled with zeenite gas, which means —"

Freddie was interrupted by his own invention. The pre-set alarm rang. The lights in the studio dimmed and the dance music began to play. The words "Random Dancing!" flashed across the *iCarly* viewers' computer screens, followed by a booming voice that ordered everyone to do the same thing.

Freddie grimaced.

Carly and Sam started dancing around wildly while Freddie tried to participate. Dancing wasn't really his thing, but Carly and Sam more than made up for him. They were having a great time, waving their arms and legs. Shaking their heads and acting crazy. They banged into each other and into Freddie.

One of them banged a little too hard.

The lightbulb flew out of Freddie's hand and smashed into the ground. The zeenite gas filled the room with a hissing sound, just before the music stopped.

Freddie picked up the smashed lightbulb with a horrified expression.

Carly and Sam stopped dancing.

"Okay, Freddie," Carly said, letting him know he could start talking again.

But by then the zeenite gas had filled the studio. And it totally stunk up the room. Carly wrinkled her nose. "Aw, man," she said.

Sam took a big sniff, and then looked like she wanted to gag. "What is that smell?" she asked.

"Zeenite gas," Freddie said sadly. "You guys made me drop my bulb and it broke." He was totally bummed. "Tech Time with Freddie" was ruined.

"Go get that fan!" Carly yelled at him. They had to clear the air — it was awful!

"And open a window. Your bulb smells worse than your socks!" Sam added.

Carly turned to the camera. "Okay, while we

de-stinkify the studio, please enjoy this video sent in by one of our *iCarly* viewers, who enjoys tick-ling himself!"

Freddie turned on the fan while Sam hit a but-ton on her remote control. The monitor on the wall sprang to life, and a video began to play.

The kid in the video was tickling his feet and laughing hysterically. "iCarly-dot-com," he said, screaming with laughter. "iCarly-dot-com!"

Just watching him laugh his head off was funny. Sam and Carly couldn't help but laugh themselves, and soon they were tickling each other and laugh-ing even harder.

The tickling boy even made Marilyn crack up downstairs. "This tickling kid is hilarious," she told Spencer.

Spencer pulled himself away from his sculp-ture and sat on the couch next to her to watch the show over her shoulder. He cracked up, too. "His laughter is contagious," he said.

"iCarly-dot-com," the kid said again, through peals of laughter.

Freddie turned off the video and turned his camera on the girls again.

"Okay, that's enough tickling," Carly said to the camera. "And it still really smells in here."

"Thanks to Freddie," Sam added, waving her hand under his nose.

Freddie glared at her. It wasn't his fault! Someone had crashed into him. Probably Sam.

"We're going to move on to our next segment," Carly said.

Sam took over the introduction. "Which we call . . ."

The girls leaned in and announced the title together. "'Fun with Bacon!'" they sang. They each held up a piece of bacon — bacon that had been decorated with tiny faces and were wearing little fringed sombreros!

Their new segment was cut short when a gas company worker burst through the door of the studio, wearing a yellow hard hat.

He checked a handheld meter. The meter's needle sprang to life when he entered the room. "This is the source," he said.

Chapter 4

Carly, Sam, and Freddie watched in stunned silence. A second gas company worker burst into the room behind the first.

"Okay, everybody out of here right now," he ordered. "Get down to the lobby."

"Why?" Carly asked, totally confused. A third man rushed through the door.

Freddie noticed that the third man seemed to be in charge. "What's going on?" he asked him.

"There's some kind of unusual gas leak coming from this room," the man said.

Carly was so shocked that she had kind of forgotten they were doing a live show for a second. Now she looked into the camera and held up a finger. "Just a sec," she told her viewers.

Freddie realized what the unusual gas was. "Oh, that was just my lightbulb," he explained. He knew zeenite gas was harmless, except for

the fact that it stunk up the room. "See, it broke and —"

The man from the gas company didn't want to hear Freddie's explanation. "All you kids. Out," he ordered.

"We can't leave!" Carly told him.

"We're halfway to breaking a world record here!" Sam said, backing up her friend.

Just then the alarm went off, the lights dimmed and then began to flash, and the deep voice intoned, "Random Dancing!"

Carly and Sam looked at each other and then did what the voice told them to do. They started to dance. The confused men from the gas company began a dance of their own.

"Why are we dancing randomly?" one of them asked.

Carly shouted so she could be heard over the music. "We can't stop our Webcast or we'll be disqualified!"

"And we won't get in the book with the fat man!" Sam explained. That was what was really important. Maybe they could even share a page with the fat man.

"Fat man?" asked the man from the gas company.

The music stopped, and the lights came up again.

Carly stopped dancing and turned to Sam. "Forget the fat man!" she yelled. Then she pleaded with the man who had ordered them to leave. "We have to stay here!"

"You're going to ruin our world record!" Freddie told him.

"I don't give a flying fishdoodle about your world record! All of you, down to the lobby, right now!" he ordered.

The *iCarly* team eyed each other, totally upset and panicked. They had come too far to stop now. They knew the gas was harmless, but arguing with the men from the gas company got them nowhere.

"There is a gas leak! You guys have got to get out of here!" one of them said.

"Wait!" Carly pleaded. She turned to the camera. "Okay, we're still in the middle of trying to break the record for world's longest continuous Webcast," she said.

"Which we will do," Sam added with utter determination.

"So right now, please enjoy the following argument." Carly turned from the camera back to the gas company representative. "We can't stop this Webcast!"

"We're trying to break a world record!" Sam told him.

Carly knew they were in no danger. She just had to try — again! — to convince the gas company that there was nothing to worry about. "There's no gas leak!" she insisted.

Sam agreed. "It was just a stinky lightbulb!"

"There's a gas leak!" the man said again. "I don't know what caused it."

But Carly did know what caused it — the lightbulb. Why wouldn't he listen? "There's no reason for us to leave!" she insisted.

"You three need to get out of here," a man from the gas company said.

Sam shook her head. She wasn't budging. "Can't you go bother some other children?"

"This is serious business. I mean it. Out!" the man ordered.

Spencer ran into the studio from downstairs. Marilyn had just told him that something was wrong.

"Okay, what's going on?" Spencer asked. He had run up two flights of stairs at top speed and could hardly breathe.

"This old dude's trying to make us leave!" Sam told him.

The man from the gas company tried to calm everybody down — including himself. "Just for a few minutes until we determine if it's dangerous or not." It took a minute for Sam's words to register. Now he was insulted. "Old dude?"

Marilyn had walked in behind Spencer.

"Is it okay if we stop our Webcast just for a few minutes?" Carly asked.

Marilyn shook her head. "I'm sorry, but if you stop I'll have to disqualify you."

Carly turned back to the camera. "Okay, people, we're having some issues here, but just keep watching *iCarly*. We're not going off the air until we break the world record."

The man from the gas company was just as

determined as Carly and Sam. He looked at his watch. "If you kids are not out of this room within thirty seconds —"

Carly didn't want to hear whatever he was about to threaten them with. She cut him off. "Freddie, can you keep the Webcast going down in the lobby?" she asked.

Freddie's mind raced from one potential problem to another. "Sort of," he said. "I'm good on camera battery, but the one in my laptop won't hold a charge. It's got to stay plugged in."

"We'll keep it plugged in!" Carly said.

"How?" Freddie asked.

"I'll handle it!" Carly yelled into the camera.

Sam echoed her. "She'll handle it!" she told Freddie. Then she turned to Carly. "How are you going to handle it?"

"I'll handle it!" Carly said again. Honestly she had no idea. But she knew she had better come up with one — fast.

The man from the gas company hadn't taken his eyes off his watch. "You've got ten seconds to get out of here," he warned.

Freddie looked at his equipment. "Help me get the stuff!" he yelled.

"Move!" Sam yelled. She plowed past the gas company workers to get to Freddie's laptop and control panel, practically knocking two of them to the floor.

Spencer and Sam helped Freddie, while Carly went in search of extension cords. Many, many extension cords. Marilyn kept monitoring the show on her laptop, to make sure they didn't stop streaming their broadcast.

A few minutes later, Marilyn followed Carly, Sam, Freddie, and Spencer as they made their way down the stairs to the lobby. Freddie kept the video camera rolling. Spencer and Sam struggled to carry a cart down the stairs. There would be no way of keeping the laptop plugged in if they took the elevator.

Carly kept up a running explanation for the *iCarly* viewers. They could not go off the air for even a *second* if they wanted to get that world record, and they had come too far to turn back now! At the same time, Carly was unrolling dozens

of extension cords that she had wrapped around her arm.

"Okay!" she said into the camera. "You're now witnessing the very first ever *iCarly* Webcast to go completely mobile."

"This is heavy," Spencer groaned. He was bearing most of the weight of the cart.

"Thanks to three dozen extension cords of various colors and girths," Sam explained to their viewers.

Spencer was in too much pain to make nice for the audience. Each step was getting harder and harder. If he relaxed even for a second, the cart would barrel down the stairs — after it crushed him, of course. "So, so heavy," he groaned again.

"We're currently moving down the back stairwell of the building," Carly told the audience.

Spencer was really struggling now. "It's hurting me."

"We're on our way to the lobby where this Webcast will continue, uninterrupted," Sam said into the camera.

They managed to get the heavy cart down all eight flights of stairs. Spencer let it down off the last step, and the cart was safely on the landing. He slumped into the wall, totally exhausted.

"Okay, we're down!" Carly said.

"We did it!" Sam added.

Just then the gas company workers came to the top of the stairs, looking considerably less stressed than they had earlier.

"Okay! The building's all clear," the workman said. "You can come back up."

The *iCarly* team exchanged tired, frustrated looks. They told the gas company guys eight long flights of stairs ago that the building was all clear. Now they had to get upstairs again, and the only way to do it while staying on the air was to make sure Freddie's laptop stayed plugged in. That meant getting the heavy cart back upstairs — one stair at a time. Without saying a word, they lifted it and started up again.

"And now . . ." Sam said into the camera.

"We go back up!" Carly finished. She started wrapping the extension cords around her arm.

42

Once more Spencer had to do most of the heavy lifting. With each step, he let out a groan. "Oh, this is worse," he said, as the cart landed on the first step with a thump. "I hate this cart. It was more fun coming down."

Chapter 5

Carly wondered if their viewers would stick with them for the long trek back up eight flights of stairs. Then she reminded herself that to win the world record, they just had to keep broadcasting. The size of their audience didn't matter. They didn't have to be interesting and funny every single second. Still, she didn't want to bore the people who watched *iCarly* every week and were rooting for them. She knew that more than a few of their regular viewers planned to stick it out with them for the entire twenty-four hours and eight minutes.

They had finally made it upstairs. Carly, Sam, and Freddie managed to keep the show going, but by the small hours of the morning, they were all getting pretty tired.

"Okay, we've been coming to you live and

uninterrupted for eighteen hours and forty-eight minutes," Carly said.

"Which means we've only got five hours and twenty-one minutes left to go," Sam added.

"Before we break the world record," Carly finished.

Spencer and Marilyn were watching the show on the computer in the kitchen downstairs. Spencer was hungry. He was also crushing on Marilyn.

He turned to her with a smile. "So c'mon, how about you and me go get some blintzes?"

"Blintzes?" Marilyn asked.

"Yeah, they're thin, sweet pancakes filled with soft cheese, usually served with jelly or jam," Spencer smiled.

Marilyn knew what blintzes were. But she also knew that Spencer was trying to do more than get her to eat. He was trying to flirt. He had been trying to flirt with her all day.

"I told you, I have a boyfriend," she said.

"Yeah, well, is he filled with soft cheese? Is he served with jelly or jam?" Spencer asked sarcastically.

45

"C'mon, don't be like that. He's a really good guy," Marilyn said. "Actually I met him through work. He holds a world record."

Now Spencer was really jealous. "For what?" he asked.

"Going the longest amount of time without blinking," Marilyn answered proudly.

That wasn't such a cool record. "Not blinking?" he asked. "Well, I can do that." He opened his eyes wide and stared at her.

"Spencer —" Marilyn said.

"Wait, I blinked. Here I go," Spencer said again.

Marilyn laughed. "You can't break his record," she said.

Spencer tried again. "Yes, I can." But he couldn't. "Darn, I blinked!" Spencer said. Once again, he opened his eyes wide. "And starting now."

But he blinked.

"Okay, now!" Spencer said.

Marilyn shook her head with a laugh.

"Wait!" Spencer told her. "Now!"

Marilyn sighed. She had a feeling Spencer was not going to give up anytime soon.

By five o'clock in the morning, the *iCarly* team had gone from kind of tired to very sleepy to totally zonked. All they could think about was sleep. The digital clock on the wall let them know that they still had four hours and eighteen minutes left to go.

Freddie wobbled on his feet, yawning behind the camera.

Carly and Sam were seated at a small table. They could hardly keep their eyes open.

"Hi," Carly murmured into the camera.

"We're tired," Sam added.

"So, what are we doing next, Sam?" Carly asked.

"I don't know," Sam mumbled. Then she realized they were sitting at a table full of makeup. She tried to think about what they were doing before they got too tired to remember anything. "Makeovers," she said.

"Oh, yeah. Makeovers," Carly answered.

They each grabbed a lipstick and, with their eyes almost closed, tried to paint each other's lips.

Carly ended up smearing Mocha Madness all over Sam's upper lip. Sam used California Coral to give Carly a pink mustache and beard.

"Ta-daaaaaa," they mumbled together, too tired to even see what they had done to each other.

"Aren't we pretty?" Carly asked the camera.

"I feel like a princess," Sam mumbled. "Now what?" she asked Carly.

"Uhhhhh," Carly said, trying to buy time while she got her brain to work again. "Let's go live to Spencer downstairs, working on his sculpture."

"Wheeeee!" Sam said, pushing the button on her remote control. Her pretend enthusiasm wasn't fooling anyone.

The TV monitor in the studio came to life at the same time as the live cam that was focused on Spencer. Carly and Sam saw that Spencer was leaning on his sculpture. He was sound asleep — standing up!

"And he's asleep," Carly mumbled.

"I'll wake him up." Sam rested her head on the table for a moment, then struggled to her feet. "Freddie, throw me the duct tape," she said.

He threw it to her. Sam caught it and picked up an air horn that was in the corner of the studio.

"Hit the elevator button," she told Carly.

Carly stumbled over to the elevator and did as she was told. She was too tired to ask Sam what she was doing.

Sam squeezed the air horn, filling the loft with an obnoxious, loud blare. Then she used the duct tape to keep the button down and the super-loud sound on. When the elevator doors opened, she threw the air horn onto it and pressed the button for the loft's first floor.

When the elevator doors closed, Carly and Sam turned to the monitor to watch Spencer.

Downstairs the elevator bell dinged and the doors opened, filling the first floor with the air-horn's long, monstrous blare.

Marilyn covered her ears.

Spencer jumped and staggered around the room, still half-asleep and trying to find the

source of the noise. Pieces of his sculpture went flying. He grabbed a plastic bat and ran toward the elevator, totally confused as to what was going on. But the elevator doors closed before he could find what was making the noise.

Sam was waiting to turn off the air horn when the elevator traveled back upstairs.

Another half hour later, the *iCarly* team was completely exhausted. Carly and Sam had to hold on to each other to stand up in front of the camera. And they still had three hours and thirty-nine minutes to go.

Freddie was so unsteady on his feet that the camera wobbled back and forth.

"Uhhhh," Carly said with a big yawn. "Next we're going to have —"

She was cut off by a familiar alarm. The lights dimmed and then began to flash. The voice-over boomed the words "Random Dancing!"

Carly and Sam both groaned, but they followed orders, dancing as wildly as their exhausted bodies would allow. In other words, not wildly at

all. Carly could barely pick her feet up, and Sam didn't seem to be able to lift her arms. When the music ended, both girls fell to the floor with a thud.

Freddie stood over them with his camera.

"Doing this Webcast is getting difficult," Sam said.

Carly remembered something. "But luckily we planned for this," she said. "We've got the perfect way to stay awake."

Sam groaned. She knew what Carly had planned and she didn't want to do it. She didn't even want to get up off the floor.

Carly struggled to her feet and grabbed a hold of Sam's long, blond, curly hair. She tugged Sam to a sort of standing position.

"And now . . ." Carly said into the camera.

Sam had her back to the camera. "We're going to stick our heads in tubs of ice water," she mumbled.

Carly spun Sam around to face the camera.

"We're going to stick our heads in tubs of ice water," Sam mumbled again.

"To keep ourselves awake," Carly explained.

The girls walked over to a table that held two giant tubs filled with ice-cold water.

Carly and Sam stood behind the table.

"On three," Carly said. "One. Two. Three."

Carly took a deep breath and then plunged her head into one of the plastic tubs. Sam did the same in the other. They held their heads under water for a few seconds and then popped up again.

"Whooooo!" Carly said, her teeth chattering.

"Whoa, daddy!" Sam exclaimed, grabbing a towel. "That woke us up!"

She was right. Both of them had a lot more energy than they did before the icy plunge. Even Freddie was feeling more alert just watching them.

Carly was wide-awake and ready to start the next segment. "And now on *iCarly*, our next guest is the only person we know who actually likes to be awake at five-thirty in the morning."

"He drove here all the way from Yakima," Sam added.

"My granddad!" Carly announced.

Sam hit the button on her remote that filled the studio with applause and cheers.

Carly's granddad ran into the room and waved to the camera. There was no question that he was awake and raring to go. "Good morning, Carly," he said. "Sam."

"How are you so awake this morning?" Carly asked.

"Yeah, what is wrong with you?" Sam joked.

"I have lots of energy because every morning I exercise," he explained. He bounced on his feet. "And who doesn't love exercise?"

"Uh, that would be most Americans," Carly told him, only half-joking.

"And that's the problem," her granddad said. "When you kids are my age, don't you want to be able to do this?" He gave himself a little drumroll and then did a handstand. He walked all around the studio — on his hands!

Carly had never seen him do that before. "Wow, pretty impressive, Granddad," she said.

"And nice socks," Sam said, noticing his bright argyles.

"Thanks! I could do this all day," Carly's grand-dad said.

He was following the sound of Sam's voice. His high energy was starting to get to her after she had spent so many hours in the studio. In fact, it was pretty annoying. She hit the elevator button and the doors opened with a ding.

"That's great. Wonderful," Sam told him. "Just keep coming over here this way."

He walked on his hands right onto the elevator, not realizing that Sam was trying to get rid of him. "See, if you girls would do a little more exercise and eat plenty of fiber —"

The elevator doors closed, taking Carly's granddad and his exercise lecture down to Spencer in the kitchen.

"And that was Carly's granddad," Sam said into the camera.

Carly was relieved. She loved her granddad, but she didn't exactly want to subject the *iCarly* viewers to one of his lectures on fiber and why it was good for you.

iCarly's 50th web show
spectacular

Chapter 6

The plunge into the ice buckets and the visit from Carly's granddad had given everyone on the *iCarly* team a second wind.

The clock continued counting down while Carly and Sam introduced a few more segments and videos. Finally, there were just four minutes and eighteen seconds remaining. It was almost time to bring the show to an end, and they had a supertastic finish planned for their audience.

"Now, since we're less than five minutes away from breaking the world record," Sam announced.

"It's time for our grand finale!" Carly said.

"That means big ending," Sam said into the camera.

"Thank you, Sam," Carly said with a confused expression. Did Sam really think their viewers

didn't know the meaning of the word "grand"? Or "finale"? She turned back to the camera. "So now, take a look at my brother, Spencer's . . ."

Carly and Sam leaned into the camera. ". . . completed sculpture!" they said together.

Sam hit the applause button on her remote, and Carly hit the elevator button.

The doors opened, and Spencer rolled his Supertastic Sculpture of Stuff off the elevator into the middle of the studio.

Carly clapped her hands. "Impressive!"

"Fabulous!" Sam said.

Freddie smiled and focused in on some of the odder objects Spencer had included, then pulled back to show the viewers the entire sculpture. It was taller than Spencer, and it was put together from all kinds of colorful, wacky objects, like a mannequin's arm, cheerleader pompoms, a lampshade, multiple pinwheels, paper stars, a party hat, toys, and anything else Spencer had found in his plastic bins . . . even the pushpins! It was truly supertastic.

"Thank you, Carly. Sam," Spencer said. "But you've seen nothing yet."

"Nothing?" Carly asked.

"Yet," Spencer said. He picked up the power cord connected to the sculpture, and walked over to an electrical outlet. "See, this isn't just a sculpture of a bunch of random items," he said. He plugged in the cord and walked back over to his creation. "This is a sculpture of a bunch of random items that move!"

Spencer flipped a switch and his crazy sculpture came to life. Dozens of parts spun, wiggled, flashed, and blinked.

"You see that?" Spencer said into the camera. "You've got all your basic movements happening here. You've got your back and forth, your to and fro, your willy and your nilly," Spencer exclaimed. "Over one hundred thirty-seven moving parts!"

"Amazing!" Carly said. "How did you decide to take all this —"

She stopped talking when the room lights flickered. The motors on the sculpture buzzed and whirred. They slowed down, and then speeded up again. The lights flickered some more.

Something was definitely wrong.

"Uh, what's going on with the lights here?" Sam asked.

Freddie ran over to his laptop and hit a couple of buttons. They were losing power! "Hey, how much electricity does that thing draw?" he asked Spencer.

Spencer looked at his sculpture. Clearly he had no clue about how much power it used. "Uhhhh, a bunch," he said.

His sculpture was way too much for the loft's electrical system. It couldn't supply power to Spencer's sculpture and to everything else at the same time. The system overloaded. The power went out, plunging the *iCarly* studio into darkness.

"The power!" Carly yelled, totally panicked.

"Unplug the sculpture!" Freddie yelled, equally panicked. If they went off the air, they would lose the world record.

"Hurry!" Sam shouted.

"Spencer!" Carly screamed.

Spencer dove for the outlet, yanking the plug out of the socket. The lights in the studio came

58

back on full strength. "Okay, okay. Problem solved," Spencer said.

But Carly wasn't so sure. "Freddie?" she asked nervously.

Freddie checked his equipment. Then he eyed the countdown clock. "We were down for about four seconds," he said seriously.

"Well, that's not a problem," Carly said. She turned to Marilyn. "Right?"

Marilyn clearly felt awful for them, but the rules were the rules. Going off the air for four seconds was a serious problem. "I'm sorry, guys. To break the world record, your Webcast had to be continuous," she said reluctantly.

"*Noooooo!*" Sam moaned.

"C'mon!" Freddie whined.

"Haven't you ever heard of the five-second rule?" Carly asked Marilyn.

Marilyn shook her head. "That's for eating food off the floor."

"Well, I feel that rule could apply here nicely," Carly said hopefully.

"I'm really sorry," Marilyn said.

"Wait," Spencer said to Carly and Sam. "I'll fix this." He edged over to Marilyn and led her a few feet away from the camera before pulling out his wallet. "Don't you think you can overlook those four unfortunate seconds when the power went down?" he asked, slipping something into her hand.

"The world record book doesn't take bribes," Marilyn said. She looked down, expecting to see cash in her hand. But that's not what Spencer had given her. "Especially not Skee-Ball tickets," she said.

"Oh, I need those," Spencer said, snatching them back. "Twenty more of these and I get a gigantic harmonica."

Carly turned to the camera, totally bummed. "Well, sorry, we didn't break the world record," she said.

"So much for getting our picture in the book with the fat man," Sam muttered.

"We'll see you here next time on *iCarly*," Carly said into the camera.

Freddie did a close-up on the clock as the time

remaining counted down to 00:00:00. "And we're out," he said. He was as bummed as Carly and Sam were.

They had lost the world record with just a couple of minutes to go.

Chapter 7

The next day Carly and her friends were sprawled out on the couch in her living room, trying to catch up on their rest. They were still tired *and* still depressed about losing the record after coming so close.

Spencer had wheeled his sculpture back downstairs and was tweaking it. He tried to cheer up the *iCarly* team.

"You guys," he said. "You're making me feel guilty here, like the whole thing was my fault."

All three of them turned to stare at Spencer. Did he seriously just say that? It was totally his fault!

"Oh, yeah," he said quietly, realizing that it was.

The doorbell rang. Spencer was the only one in the room with enough energy to answer it. He ran over and opened the door to find Marilyn, along with a man with incredibly wide, bugged-out eyes.

"Marilyn," Spencer said.

Carly, Sam, and Freddie sat up.

"Hi, Spencer," Marilyn said. "This is my boyfriend, Calvin."

"The guy who never blinks?" Spencer asked.

"That's right," Calvin said. There was a challenge in his voice. He obviously knew all about Spencer's lame attempts to break his record.

Spencer snapped his fingers and clapped his hands in Calvin's face, trying to get him to blink.

"Not a chance," Calvin told him.

"Hi, Marilyn," Carly said.

"Hi, Carly."

"What's up?" Carly asked.

"Well, even though you guys didn't break the record for the world's longest continuous Webcast," Marilyn said, "I did a little research, and Spencer did break a record."

"Huh?" Spencer asked.

Marilyn opened the *Jonas Book of World Records*. "The world record for Most Moving

Pieces on a Sculpture is one hundred and twenty-eight moving parts."

"But mine's got one hundred and thirty-seven," Spencer said. "That's more."

"He's an artist, and he's also a math whiz," Sam said sarcastically.

Carly's dark mood lifted a little. "So you're saying Spencer broke a world record?" she asked.

Marilyn nodded. "That's exactly what I'm saying."

"Oh my gosh, you get to be in the world record book!" Carly said, totally excited for him.

Even Sam was happy for him. If she couldn't be in the book, she was glad to know Spencer would be in there with the fat man. "Way to go, Spence," she said.

"Good job, Spencer," Freddie added.

Marilyn held up her camera. "If I could just take a picture of you with your sculpture, I can get it all processed in time for the next edition of the book."

"Sweet!" Spencer said. He hurried over to the sculpture and struck a pose. "Make sure my hair is parted right," he said.

Just as Marilyn was about to snap the picture, he stopped her. "Wait! What if I'm not the only person who worked on the sculpture?" he asked.

"The rules say that all participants would have to get credit," Marilyn said.

Spencer broke into a big grin. "Carly, Sam, Freddie," he said, waving them over to him.

"What?" they asked.

"Well, I . . ." Spencer looked around. He grabbed his cordless drill. "I forgot this one last piece to the sculpture, and my hands are really sore," he said. "Would you guys mind putting it on there for me?"

The *iCarly* team realized what Spencer was doing. He was making sure their pictures would be included in the book, too. He might have ruined the *iCarly* team's world record attempt, but now he was making sure they got one after all.

"We can do that," Carly said, grinning back.

"Let's help our friend Spencer finish the sculpture," Freddie said.

Carly, Sam, and Freddie took the drill and added it to the sculpture together.

"Right there," Spencer directed. "Get it in there good."

They stepped back from the sculpture and admired it. Now it had one hundred and thirty-eight moving parts.

"Perfect," Spencer said. He looked at Marilyn and pretended to be surprised. "Wait, since they helped me finish the sculpture, I guess we all have to get credit and be in the picture," he said innocently.

"Those are the rules," Marilyn said with a smile. "Ready?"

Carly, Sam, and Freddie stood with Spencer in front of the sculpture. Marilyn raised the camera and snapped the picture.

"Wait, I think I blinked," Spencer said.

"I didn't," Calvin said with a smug expression.

"I can see why you love him," Spencer said to Marilyn.

Marilyn smiled again. "Oh, and I have another little surprise for Sam," she said. "Mr. McGurthey?" she called out the front door.

"Coming . . ." said a voice from the hall.

Sam's jaw dropped. She knew that name. "No way!" she yelled. "The world's fattest man?"

"He's here?" Carly asked.

Marilyn nodded. "He is. Coming down the hallway right —"

There was a horrible crashing noise and a scream from the hall. Marilyn looked outside, and then turned back to them with a horrified expression. "He fell through the floor!"

They all ran out into the hall to see if he was okay. Maybe they could even break a new world record — the fewest number of people to help the world's fattest man to his feet.

iGot
Detention

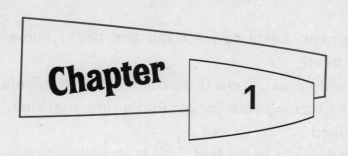

Chapter 1

Carly was hanging out in the hall in between her classes. A group of her classmates were laughing about something that happened over the weekend when Mr. Howard, a super-mean teacher, walked by.

Mr. Howard could not stand the sound of laughter or the idea of anyone having fun. Carly thought it must be because he never had any fun himself.

"No laughing," he yelled, pointing at the kids.

They quickly stepped out of his way. *Since when couldn't you laugh in the hall?* they wondered.

"I don't like children," Mr. Howard muttered as he made his way up the stairs.

What a surprise, Carly thought sarcastically. She shook her head. Teachers could be so weird. Who could figure out their random rules?

Then she spotted Freddie kneeling in front of his locker. He was surrounded by high-tech

equipment. Carly saw a flash and heard something beep.

"Freddie, you know this school has a strict rule against turning your locker into a time machine," she joked.

Freddie got to his feet. "It's a surveillance system," he said.

Freddie was spying on the inside of his locker? "For?" Carly asked.

"Someone snuck into my locker yesterday and stole my fruit-scented markers," Freddie said, totally outraged.

Carly slipped her backpack off her shoulders and started rummaging inside while Freddie explained how his burglar alarm system worked.

"So the next time someone breaks in, it'll trigger this mechanism," he said, pointing at a switch he had hooked up to his locker door, "which causes this camera to snap a picture of the thief." The camera flashed, taking Freddie's picture.

Carly found what she was looking for. She pulled a box out of her backpack and tried to hand it to Freddie.

He was still explaining his surveillance

system. "So I'll know —" Freddie stopped talking when he saw what was in Carly's hand. "That you took my markers!" he said.

"Sorry, I forgot to tell you," Carly said.

"How did you pick my lock?" Freddie asked.

Freddie answered his own question at the same time as Carly did. "Sam," they both said together.

"Of course," Freddie said with a nod. Who else did Carly hang out with who would know how to pick a lock? He took his box of fruit-scented markers. There was one missing. "Hey, where's the tangerine one?" he asked.

"I'm not sure," Carly answered, not looking him in the eye.

Freddie sighed and put the markers back in his locker. What if he needed just that color? As soon as his back was turned, Carly pulled the tangerine-scented marker out of her back pocket, uncapped it, and took a big sniff. She loved that smell! She couldn't give the marker back.

It was safely capped and back in her pocket before Freddie turned around again.

"So what did you need the markers for?" Freddie asked.

"To make that poster," Carly said, pointing to a sign that Sam was putting up on a bulletin board.

"Oh yeah," Freddie said, reading the poster. "*iCarly* Fiftieth Web Show Spectacular."

The *iCarly* team was hoping for their biggest audience yet. Carly and Sam had worked really hard on the poster. Well, Carly had. Sam had watched.

"Cool," Freddie said. "Spreading the word."

"And the smell of fruits," Carly joked.

Sam walked over and joined them. She admired the sign from across the hall. "There, it's up," she said. "Can you guys believe we're about to shoot our fiftieth Webcast of *iCarly*?"

"Insane," Freddie said.

The three of them never guessed that their show would be such a big hit. At first, they just wanted to have some fun and show the world some of their classmates' wacky talents. Talents that Miss Briggs had refused to put in the talent show, like pogo-stick hopping while trumpet playing, and being able to say everything

backwards. Since their first broadcast, the show had really taken off. They had fans from all over the world!

"We've got to make it like our best show ever," Carly said.

Sam nodded. "No doubt."

Just then two football players, Chuck and Dave, walked by. Sam snatched Chuck's football. "Hey, Chuck, go long!" Sam yelled.

"Okay!" Chuck ran all the way up the stairs and paused at the top.

Sam threw a good, strong spiral pass. The only problem was that, instead of landing in Chuck's outstretched hands, it nailed Mr. Howard right in the face.

Mr. Howard let out a pained yelp and tumbled down the stairs. Carly, Sam, and Freddie ran over to him, along with everyone else in the hall. The teacher lay in a heap on the floor with his hands over his face. He didn't make a sound.

They all wondered what to do. But then Carly's friend Gibby noticed the *iCarly* poster, and Mr. Howard was quickly forgotten.

"Oh my gosh," Gibby said. "*iCarly*'s having a Fiftieth Web Show Spectacular?"

"Yeah," Carly said with a smile.

Everyone ran over to the sign, chatting about their favorite episodes. Mr. Howard was left on the floor by himself, completely motionless.

"That's awesome!" Gibby said.

"I love *iCarly*," said another guy.

"I can't wait!" someone else said.

The bell rang and they all scattered to class. All of them except Mr. Howard.

Later that day, Sam found herself in a familiar place — the principal's office. Principal Franklin sat at his desk. The computer screen behind him held a picture of the school mascot — the Ridgeway bulldog.

Sam sat across from the principal while Mr. Howard furiously paced back and forth. Sam thought briefly that Mr. Howard would make an excellent bulldog, but then she quickly put the thought out of her mind before she started to laugh.

Mr. Howard was obviously way too angry to sit down. He wore headgear because of his injury. A yellow piece of plastic cupped his chin, another piece stretched across his forehead, and metal wires held the whole cockamamie contraption all together. It was like a cross between a night brace and a cast, and it was making it very hard for Mr. Howard to talk. Or yell.

"This girl is a menace! I want her expelled!" Mr. Howard said.

Only it sounded like, "This girl is a memace. I want her esspelt."

"What?" Principal Franklin asked.

"I want her esspelt!" Mr. Howard repeated.

"What?" Principal Franklin asked again.

The teacher's words were still distorted, but Sam understood Mr. Howard perfectly. She was used to having teachers demand that she be expelled. It happened all the time. This wasn't even the first time *Mr. Howard* had wanted her expelled! "He wants me expelled," she told the principal.

Principal Franklin was used to the demand as well, but he was always able to talk her teachers

in to more reasonable punishments. Of course, Sam had never done bodily harm to a teacher before.

"Mr. Howard, c'mon," Principal Franklin said. "I realize it was wrong of Sam to throw a football in the hallway —"

Mr. Howard cut him off before the principal could come to Sam's defense. "She almost killed me!" he said.

"Yeah," Sam agreed. "*Almost*." Almost was the key word, wasn't it?

"I want something done about this!" Mr. Howard demanded.

"I understand," Principal Franklin told him. But Mr. Howard's headgear was still making it difficult to understand him. "Sort of," he admitted. Then the principal turned to Sam with a sigh. "Sam, you did break the rules."

Mr. Howard muttered something and nodded. He waited for Principal Franklin to throw the book at Sam.

Sam braced herself.

"So, I'm going to give you detention with

Mr. Howard tomorrow night," Principal Franklin said.

Sam rolled her eyes. Not a big deal. She was used to detention. "Fine, I'll be there tomorr —" Suddenly Sam realized that Principal Franklin was giving her detention on the very same night as the Fiftieth Web Show Spectacular. "Wait, I can't do it tomorrow night," she said.

"Why not?" the principal asked.

"Yeah, why not?" Mr. Howard asked.

"Because I do a Web show," Sam said.

"I know," Principal Franklin said with a nod. *"iCarly."*

Mr. Howard had never heard of it. *"iCarly?"* he asked.

"Yeah, and tomorrow night's our fiftieth Webcast, and it's going to be, like, a big thing, you know?" Sam explained.

Principal Franklin's intercom beeped. He pressed the button. "Yes?"

"Principal Franklin, some ninth grade boys are giving Gibby a wedgie," his secretary said over the intercom.

"Again?" Principal Franklin sighed. "All right. I'll be right there," he said, heading for the door. "Mr. Howard, you finish up here."

Sam knew she was in trouble now. Principal Franklin was way nicer and way more reasonable than Mr. Howard. She tried to keep him in the room with her. "Wait, just don't —"

But the principal didn't hear her, or didn't care. He was already out of the room. He had a wedgie emergency to deal with.

Sam was alone with Mr. Howard, the teacher who tried to ban laughter in the halls. The teacher who she hit in the face with a football. The teacher who wanted her expelled.

Mr. Howard glared at her.

It's time for some sucking up, Sam thought. "You know, I think you look better with that thing on your face," she said.

It didn't work.

"Be quiet!" Mr. Howard barked.

"Okay," Sam agreed. "But can I please do detention next week?" she pleaded.

"What, you think just because you're on a

popular Web show, that you deserve some special treatment?" Mr. Howard asked.

Sam nodded. "Yeah."

"Well, tough kumquats!" Mr. Howard said.

"Tough what?" Sam asked.

"Kumquats!" Mr. Howard screamed.

Sam still didn't understand him. "What?"

Totally frustrated, Mr. Howard yanked his headgear off, threw it to the floor, and stomped on it. "Kumquats! Kumquats! Kumquats!" he screamed. He cupped his jaw, obviously in a lot of pain, and muttered unintelligible threats in Sam's direction as he stormed out of the office.

Sam was still confused. "Kumquats?" she asked. But there was no one there to answer.

Chapter 2

The *iCarly* team hung out in Carly's loft after school, trying to think of a solution to their problem. They had already posted the date of the Fiftieth Web Show Spectacular in school and on the *iCarly* Website. All of their viewers knew it was scheduled for the next night. They couldn't change the date now.

"Why'd you have to get detention tomorrow night?" Carly asked, carrying a big bowl of popcorn into the living room.

"Yeah, way to go, Sam," Freddie said sarcastically. "You just ruined *iCarly*'s Fiftieth Web Show Spectacular." Then he noticed the snack in Carly's hands and he forgot all about being angry with Sam. "Oooh, popcorn!"

Sam stood by the microwave in the kitchen "You know, I read online that popcorn is one of the healthiest snacks you can eat," she said.

"Yeah, I read that too," Carly said.

The microwave beeped and Sam took a measuring cup full of yellow liquid out of the oven. She carried it into the living room and held it over the popcorn as if she was about to pour it on top.

"Whoa, whoa, what is that?" Carly asked, stopping her.

"Two cups of melted butter," Sam answered.

"Don't pour that all over the popcorn," Freddie said, totally disgusted.

Carly agreed. "It's full of fat and calories!"

"*Okaaaay*," Sam said, but it was obvious that she didn't think it was such a big deal. Popcorn and butter went together, and what was wrong with fat and calories anyway? She liked fat and calories. She looked at the measuring cup, thinking.

Carly read her thoughts. "Don't drink it!" she said.

Sam put the cup down.

Freddie was back to wondering what they could do to save *iCarly*'s big show. "Why don't you just go talk to Mr. Howard and explain that it's *iCarly*'s fiftieth?" he asked.

"Tried that, didn't work," Sam said, trying to think of a plan. "Hey, what if we kidnap and tie up Mr. Howard until after the show?" she asked.

Carly rolled her eyes. Kidnapping was one of Sam's favorite go-to ideas. It was a frequent suggestion of hers. The only problem was that it would get them arrested. "Okay, what have I told you about kidnapping?" Carly asked.

Sam recited the statement about kidnapping that Carly had made her memorize. "It's illegal and rude," she chanted.

"Good girl," Carly said, patting Sam's knee.

The elevator doors opened with a ding. Spencer rolled a wheelbarrow full of golf balls off the elevator. He was dressed in full scuba gear. "I'm home," he announced happily.

"Where've you been?" Freddie asked.

"Down at the golf course," Spencer explained. "Getting balls out of the big pond."

"What for?" Sam asked.

"So I can sell them, then buy art supplies for my next sculpture," Spencer answered.

"What are you making?" Carly asked.

"A gigantic coffee cup. Like ten feet tall," Spencer said, totally excited.

"Why?" Freddie asked.

"You know," Spencer said, "to symbolize the . . . the largeness of some coffee cups that are . . . um, big." Really he had no idea why; he just wanted to make a big coffee cup. He changed the subject. "I'm going to take a shower," he said, heading for his room, flippers, mask, and all.

"Have fun," Carly said.

Freddie got back to business. "So, what are we going to do about *iCarly*?" he asked.

"We've got to figure out a way to get Sam out of detention," Carly said.

Sam shook her head. "Not gonna happen. Mr. Howard hates my guts."

"Then maybe me and Carly need to figure out a way to get *into* detention," Freddie joked.

Sam chuckled. As if Freddie and Carly ever did anything bad enough to get detention.

But Carly was intrigued. She got to her feet, thinking. "Hey. . . ."

"What?" Sam and Freddie asked, at the same time. Carly had her "I've got a great idea" look.

"*iCarly* — live from detention," Carly said. It was perfect!

Sam thought about it for a minute. "Interesting," she said.

"Wait, you're serious?" Freddie asked.

"Sure," Carly told him. "You and I do something bad, we get detention, then the three of us will be together to do the show."

"How can we do the show with Mr. Howard watching us the whole time?" Freddie asked.

Sam was the detention expert. She knew exactly how. "He hardly ever comes in the room," she said. "He always hangs in the teacher's lounge so he can watch the Geometry Channel." She shook her head at the idea of anyone watching the Geometry Channel for fun, even a teacher. "He's such a nub."

"The nubbiest," Carly agreed.

"All right," Freddie said, coming around to the idea. "Let's do it."

"Awesome," Carly said. "So tomorrow before school ends, you and I have to get detention."

Spencer came back into the room, still wearing the bottom half of his wet suit. There was a small fish wiggling in his hand, and he looked kind of freaked out. "You'll never guess where I found this fish," he said.

The *iCarly* team stared at him, completely speechless. They didn't want to guess. They didn't even want to know.

The next morning in Social Studies, Freddie sat at his desk, nervously drumming his fingers.

Sam breezed into the room. "Hey," she said.

Freddie gave her an anxious smile. He wasn't used to being bad. "Hello, Sam," he said.

"Why do you look all guilty?" she asked.

"I did something bad," he admitted proudly. "To get detention."

"What'd you do?" Sam asked, curious about Freddie's definition of "bad."

"You'll see," he assured her.

The bell rang and their teacher, Mr. Paladino, walked into the room. "All right, class, everyone please sit," he said.

87

Freddie turned to the desk behind him and handed his friend Gibby a folder. "Gibby, go ask Mr. Paladino to staple these papers together," Freddie whispered.

"What for?" Gibby asked.

"*Shhhh!* Just do it," Freddie said.

A very confused Gibby took the papers out of the folder and carried them up to Mr. Paladino's desk. "Hey, Mr. Paladino, could you please staple these together?" he asked, handing him the papers that were in the folder.

"Certainly, Gibby."

Gibby turned to look at Freddie, still confused. Freddie gave him a big thumbs-up signal.

Mr. Paladino searched for his stapler. "Hmmm, that's odd. I don't see my stapler anywhere."

Freddie slyly showed Sam the stapler in his lap. He had taken it from Mr. Paladino's desk before anyone else got to class. "I have it," he whispered.

"Wow, you're a maniac," Sam said sarcastically.

Freddie shrugged proudly. As far as he was concerned, taking a stapler was pretty high on the bad behavior list.

Mr. Paladino was still checking his desk drawers. Then he gave up. "I'm sorry, Gibby, I can't find the stapler," he said.

Freddie cleared his throat. "That's right," he said loudly. He got to his feet and held the stapler in the air. "Because I took it." He chewed his gum and sneered like a juvenile delinquent in a really cheesy movie.

But no one would have ever cast Freddie as a juvenile delinquent, especially not his teachers.

"Oh, yes." Mr. Paladino walked over to Freddie. "Thank you, Freddie," he said, casually taking the stapler back.

Freddie slumped back into his seat with a frown. Why didn't Mr. Paladino yell at him? Why didn't he get detention?

Mr. Paladino only stapled the papers together and gave them to Gibby. "There you are, Gibby."

Gibby walked back to his desk, offering Freddie the papers as he passed by.

"Keep them," Freddie muttered.

☺ ☺ ☺ ☺ ☺

While Freddie was trying to get detention in Social Studies, Carly was trying to achieve the same goal in Math.

Carly worked on the teacher's desk chair with a socket wrench while kids milled around before class. When the bell rang, Carly scurried to her seat and waited for her teacher, Mrs. Rosenthal, to arrive.

"All right, kids, the sooner we start, the sooner we finish," Mrs. Rosenthal said, coming into the room. "So, everybody, let's take our seats."

Mrs. Rosenthal sat, and her chair immediately fell apart. The math teacher fell over backward and crashed to the floor with a thud.

"What happened to my chair?" Mrs. Rosenthal asked, getting to her feet.

Carly hopped to her feet. "I did it!" she said proudly. She waved the socket wrench in the air. "With whatever this is. Do I get detention after school today?" she asked.

Mrs. Rosenthal put a hand on her back. "Absolutely not!" she said. "An on-the-job accident means the school has to give me a two-month paid vacation while I recover! Bye!"

She grabbed her briefcase and ran out of the room. She didn't look like she had anything to recover from.

Mrs. Rosenthal's class celebrated their sudden free period, while Carly slumped at her desk, totally bummed out. She wanted detention! Instead she had gotten thanked. What was she going to do?

Chapter 3

Freddie was still determined to get detention. If stealing a stapler wasn't bad enough, he'd have to raise his badness level. Sam didn't believe he could do it, but Freddie was going to prove her wrong!

Later that day, he led Sam into the principal's office to show her his latest attempt to get into trouble.

They snuck past the principal's secretary and into the empty room.

"Dude, this is the principal's office," Sam told him. She thought Freddie might never have seen it before.

"I know! I'm so bad," Freddie said. "Look what I did."

Freddie raised the blinds covering the window to show Sam the message he had painted on Principal Franklin's window.

Sam read the message out loud. "'Freddie says: Principal Franklin smells.'" She eyed Freddie with new respect. "Impressive," she said. "That might get you double detention."

Freddie grinned proudly. "Yep. When Principal Franklin sees that, you better believe he's going to —"

At that moment, the school's gardener started to trim the hedges outside the window. He noticed the words painted there, and used his watering hose to wash the window clean. Freddie's insult was washed away before the principal could see it, along with Freddie's hopes for detention.

Meanwhile, Carly was pacing up and down the hall during lunch period. She couldn't eat. She was too nervous. She eyed the fire alarm. She reached out to pull it, and then drew her hand back. She had never done anything this bad.

"C'mon, Carly," she said to herself. "It's for the Fiftieth Web Show Spectacular. You can do this." She reached for the alarm again, then pulled her hand back.

She stretched her arm out a third time. This time her fingers actually touched the red switch, but she couldn't bring herself to push it and disrupt the whole school by setting off the fire alarm. Finally, she took her sandwich out of her lunch bag and threw it, quickly covering her ears.

Nothing happened. That's what she got for using soft bread, she thought. She'd better switch to whole wheat, or something.

Next, she took a banana out of the bag and threw that — hard. The siren blasted through the halls. Carly covered her ears and waited to get yanked to the principal's office.

A teacher, Mr. Stern, stuck his head out of the teacher's lounge. "Who pulled that fire alarm?"

"It was me," Carly admitted, ready to accept her punishment.

"Well, thank goodness you did," he said. "The microwave in the teacher's lounge just burst into flames!" He held the door open while another teacher ran out. He was wearing oven mitts and carrying the burning microwave.

"Out of the way! Out of the way!" the teacher yelled.

94

Carly watched him run outside while Mr. Stern used a key to turn off the fire alarm. She felt totally defeated. What did she have to do to get detention?

A couple of hours later, Sam and Freddie joined Carly at her locker to find out if she had managed to get in trouble. She hadn't. All of her attempts had failed.

"Who knew getting in trouble would be so impossible?" she asked, totally frustrated.

Freddie was having the same problem. "I've got to give you credit, Sam. You make it look easy," he said.

"Years of practice," Sam answered. She had made getting into trouble an art form. "And, hey, thanks for that fire alarm," she said to Carly. "You saved me from giving an oral report on *Scarlett's Web*."

"You were too lazy to read the book?" Carly asked.

"I was too lazy to see the movie," Sam answered.

Carly sighed and brought the conversation back to the problem at hand. They had told their viewers that this week's show would be spectacular, but they couldn't go on without Sam. Either Sam had to get *out* of detention, which was impossible, or Carly and Freddie had to get *into* detention. So far that was looking pretty impossible, too.

"Well, now what?" Carly asked. "We're supposed to do the fiftieth Webcast of *iCarly* from detention in" — she checked her cell phone — "five hours, and Sam's the only one who's going to be there!" She stamped her foot. "Why is it so hard to get detention?" she asked, slamming her locker closed with a loud bang.

The door to a nearby classroom opened, and Mr. Howard stuck his head out into the hall. He didn't like loud noises any more than he liked laughter. "Who slammed that locker?" he demanded.

"Me," Carly said.

He pointed at her. "Detention," he yelled.

Carly's eyes lit up with excitement. "Really?"

"Tonight," Mr. Howard ordered.

"Yay!" Carly said with a big smile.

"Yay?" Mr. Howard asked, glaring at her. Had he made someone happy? If there was one thing Mr. Howard hated, it was making people happy.

"Darn," she said, correcting herself.

Mr. Howard closed his door.

"You did it!" Sam said.

Carly was excited, but their problem was only half-solved. "Yeah, but we still need our tech producer and school's over in three minutes," she said.

"How am I going to get detention in three minutes?" Freddie asked.

"You better, or else no-show tonight," Sam said.

Just then Principal Franklin walked by talking on his cell phone. Freddie saw an opportunity.

"Wait here," he said with a determined expression. He marched over to the principal, who was in mid-conversation, and snatched his cell phone. Then Freddie threw it to the floor like he wanted to break it.

Even Sam gasped at Freddie's boldness. He would be lucky if detention was all he got.

Freddie braced himself for trouble — big trouble.

Principal Franklin only chuckled. "Oh, you heard I got the new Pear phone." He bent over to pick up the phone. "Yeah, these babies are indestructible." He banged his phone hard against a locker — three times! — to demonstrate. The phone was just fine. Principal Franklin put it to his ear. "Hello, honey," he said into the phone. "I'm back. Yes, I will pick up some donuts." He walked off to finish his conversation.

Freddie was completely and totally dumbfounded. He had just snatched the principal's cell phone and thrown it to the floor, and all the principal did was chuckle! Unbelievable! He trudged back over to Carly and Sam just as the final bell rang. That was it. He had failed in his final opportunity to get detention.

"Aw man, school's over," Carly said.

"And you didn't get detention," Sam said

"Which means no *iCarly* Fiftieth Web Show Spectacular," Carly said sadly.

Sam was convinced they faced disaster. Their

audience wouldn't trust them anymore. They'd lose their viewers. "This could *not* be worse."

"Yes it could," Freddie said defensively.

"How?" Sam asked.

Carly spotted Gibby painfully walking down the hall. *It could be worse*, she realized. "We could be Gibby," she said.

Gibby was hunched over, cringing with each step. "They gave me a wedgie," he moaned.

There was a boy with problems!

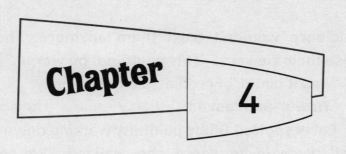

Chapter 4

The *iCarly* team headed to the Shays' loft after school to see if they could come up with a solution to their problem. Freddie stopped at his own apartment across the hall, but Carly and Sam went straight to Carly's.

Carly used her key to open the door. Both girls stopped short when they saw what was there to greet them. There was a gigantic cup of coffee in the middle of the living room. Carly had come home to plastic robots, elaborate machines, and chairs made of flip-flops, but she had never come home to anything quite this big. It was the Grand Canyon of coffee cups.

"Man, when Spencer said he was building a gigantic cup of coffee, he wasn't kidding around," Sam said, approaching it slowly.

Carly looked up at it. The cup looked exactly like a regular coffee cup, right down to the piece

of cardboard that keeps you from burning your fingers. Only this one was huge. It was almost twice Carly's height.

"Where is Spencer?" Carly asked. Then she called his name. "Hey, Spencer?"

The girls heard a sloshing sound and then saw Spencer's head pop up above the rim of the cup. He was wearing a snorkeling mask. He went under again, and then bobbed his head above the surface.

"Up here!" Spencer said, hanging onto the side of the cup. Brown liquid splashed over the side.

Carly and Sam backed away.

"Is that thing filled with coffee?" Sam asked.

"Oh, just about five hundred gallons," Spencer said proudly.

"Spencer, that's crazy!" Carly said.

Spencer laughed. "Nah, it's okay — it's decaf," he joked.

"Okay," Sam said slowly. She was more than a little confused. "But why are you in there?"

"Because, right after I filled it up with coffee, I dropped my cell phone in here," Spencer explained. "I've been trying to find it for the past

two hours. Wish me luck." He pulled his mask down and dove to the bottom of the cup. His swim fins stuck above the surface for a second and then disappeared. More coffee sloshed over the cup's rim.

Freddie knocked on the door and came in. "Hey, I figured out a way for us to do *iCarly* tonight," he said happily. Then he noticed the cup. "Is that a ten-foot tall coffee cup?"

Spencer popped above the rim again. "Ten-foot-two!" he yelled. He took a deep breath and dove back down to the bottom of the cup.

Freddie shook his head. "I'm not even going to ask," he told Carly.

"Just tell us how we're going to do the show tonight!" Carly said. That was much more important than Spencer's new creation.

"All right," Freddie said. "Is there a closet in the classroom?"

"Yeah," Sam answered.

"Good. Then you guys can hide my camera and tech equipment in there so Mr. Howard won't see it," Freddie said.

Carly was confused. They needed Freddie,

not just his equipment. Who would be their cameraman? "Yeah, but what about you?" she asked.

"You can't be in there unless you have detention," Sam said. No one *crashed* detention.

"You said Howard is almost never in the room because he's watching the Geometry Channel in the teacher's lounge, right?" Freddie asked.

"Yeah," Sam said, still not understanding.

"So, as soon as he checks roll and leaves, you guys give me a signal, and I'll sneak in the window," Freddie explained.

Now Sam and Carly were even more confused. "But the classroom's on the second floor," Carly said.

Spencer popped his head over the cup's rim again. "You can borrow my ladder," he yelled.

Problem solved! Freddie gave Spencer a smile and a thumbs-up. "Awesome!"

"Did I hear you say you got detention?" Spencer asked Carly.

"Yeah," Carly admitted.

"Should I be concerned?" Spencer asked.

"Not really," Carly said.

That was enough for Spencer. He knew Carly was a good kid. He trusted her. And right now he had a phone to find. "Later," he said, taking another deep breath and diving back down into the coffee.

Carly turned to her friends with a big grin. The *iCarly* Web Show Spectacular was definitely going to happen!

A couple of hours later, Carly, Sam, and about ten other kids faced Mr. Howard in the classroom that was being used for detention. Carly and Sam had gotten there early enough to hide Freddie's camera equipment in the closet before Mr. Howard arrived.

The teacher paced back and forth in the front of the room while he told the students exactly what he thought of them. It wasn't pretty.

"Now, you are all here because you are the worst this school has to offer," he said with a menacing sneer. "I am here because I believe in punishment and discipline."

Wow, that's harsh, Carly thought. But of course she couldn't say anything. Sam merely rolled her eyes. She had heard Mr. Howard's tirades before. By now it was just plain boring.

Mr. Howard waited for a reaction. The rest of the kids in the room wanted to tell him how they felt, but they couldn't. They were silent.

"All right," he said, satisfied. "I'll be down the hall in the teacher's lounge watching the Geometry Channel. While I'm gone, there is to be no talking. I hope you have a terrible time."

Carly and Sam watched him go. Obviously Mr. Howard enjoyed holding detention. But they wouldn't have the terrible time he wanted them to have — not tonight.

Tonight the Ridgeway School detention class would be a part of Web show history!

"We're good now for at least ten minutes," Sam told Carly.

Carly nodded. "Let's go."

Sam went to get the equipment out of the closet while Carly clued the class into what she was trying to do. "Okay, everybody, we're about to start

the fiftieth Webcast of *iCarly*. You guys into it?"
she asked.

Of course they were. The whole school loved
iCarly.

"Yeah!" someone said.

"Totally!" added Carly's friend Claire.

"Awesome!" said another.

"Okay, who wants to be the lookout?" Carly
asked.

Claire raised her hand. "I'll do it," she said,
crossing over to the door. There was a window
that allowed her to look all the way down the hall
to the door of the teacher's lounge. She'd see Mr.
Howard whenever he left the lounge to check on
them. The Geometry Channel didn't have all that
many commercials — but whenever it did, Howard
showed up to make sure they were behaving.

Sam leaned out of the closet. "Hey, go signal
Freddie," she said to Carly.

"Right!" Carly ran over to the window. She
opened it and gave Freddie the signal. "K'kaw!
K'kaw!" she said, imitating a bird.

"K'kaw!" Freddie answered, in his normal tone
of voice.

"Do it like a bird!" Carly yelled down to him. What was the fun of a secret signal if Freddie wouldn't play along?

"K'kaw!" Freddie said, making his voice higher this time and sounding more like a bird.

The top of the ladder appeared in the window, and Freddie began to climb the rungs.

"Carly, what's the signal for 'Mr. Howard's coming'?" Claire asked.

"Uh . . . dippidy-doo," Carly said, thinking fast.

"Well, dippidy-doo!" Claire said, starting to panic.

"Everybody sit back down!" Carly said, rushing to her seat.

The kids all rushed back to their chairs, but Carly had forgotten all about Freddie. He was still on the ladder. "Quick, pull me in!" he whispered.

Sam ran over from the closet. "Too late!" she said. She gave the ladder a push so that Mr. Howard wouldn't see it and ran to her seat. She got there just in time.

The sound of Freddie crashing into a bush and the painful yelp he let out was drowned out by Mr. Howard's loud voice.

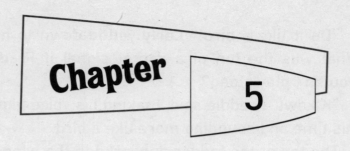

Chapter 5

Mr. Howard burst through the classroom door. "I heard noise. What's going on?" he demanded.

"Nothing," Sam said.

"We're just sitting here having a terrible time," Carly said innocently.

Together, the girls let out a big, sad sigh.

The sound of the girls' sad sighs convinced Mr. Howard. "Good. Just sit here and don't move," he snapped. Then he closed the door and headed back to the teacher's lounge.

The kids jumped to their feet. Claire took her lookout position again.

"I'll get the stuff out of the closet," Sam said.

Carly ran back to the window. "I'll get Freddie," she said. She opened the window and gave him the signal. "K'kaw."

"K'kaw," Freddie groaned. He leaned the ladder up against the side of the school again and began to climb.

Sam ran out of the closet with a fishing cap made out of camouflage material. There was a circle on the front of it, like a little window. Only it was a camera lens.

"Here, you're wearing the Cap Cam," she said, placing it on Billy's head.

"Why?" Billy asked. The cap wasn't his style.

"There's a camera in it," Sam explained. "If Mr. Howard comes back, Freddie hides in the closet and we switch *iCarly* to the hidden camera in your hat." Billy was sitting in the back row — the perfect place for the Cap Cam to catch the action.

"Cool!" Billy answered.

Freddie reached the top of the ladder. His hair was full of twigs and leaves, and he was obviously in pain. "I fell in a shrub," he moaned.

Carly helped him climb through the window.

Freddie worked on his equipment while Carly and Sam got ready to start the show.

"Coast clear?" Carly asked Claire.

Claire checked the hall. "All clear," she said.

Freddie lifted his camera to his shoulder. "And we're live on the Web in five, four, three, two. . . ." On the number one he pointed at the girls.

Carly and Sam leaned in so that their faces were right in front of the lens and screamed.

"Why did we just scream?" Carly asked.

"Because . . ." Sam answered.

Freddie hit a key on his laptop and a graphic flashed across the screen that read, "*iCarly's* 50th Web Show Spectacular." At the same time, their viewers heard the words being sung by the Jingle Singers, a group Spencer knew. They had pre-recorded some lyrics for the special show.

"It's true!" Carly said.

"This is the fiftieth Webcast of *iCarly*!" Sam added with excitement.

"And it is spectacular!" Carly assured their viewers.

Sam pressed a button on her remote and the Jingle Singers sang, "Spectacular!"

"I'm Carly," Carly said into the camera.

"And I'm Sam."

As usual, the girls switched back and forth and finished each other's sentences.

"And maybe you've noticed . . ." Carly began.

". . . this isn't our usual *iCarly* studio," Sam finished.

"And if you haven't noticed . . ." Carly said.

". . . open your eyes!" Sam joked.

Carly explained to their viewers what was going on. "We're Webcasting to you live from our school," she said.

"Room twenty-nine," Sam burst in.

Carly continued, "Because we got . . ."

Sam pressed a button on her remote and the Jingle Singers sang, "Detention!" at the same time as a graphic of the word flashed across their viewers' computer screens.

"Tell them why we got detention," Sam said.

"Because we're naughty," Carly joked.

Claire was still standing by the door, looking out for Mr. Howard. The Geometry Channel must have taken a commercial break, because she spotted him leaving the teacher's lounge. "Dippidy-doo!" she yelled.

"Uh, okay, you just heard our friend Claire yell dippidy-doo," Carly said, slightly panicked.

"Which means that our teacher Mr. Howard is coming," Sam explained.

"I've got to hide!" Freddie said. He started to back into the closet.

Carly and Sam followed him, still talking into the camera. Behind them, the kids all rushed back to their seats.

"Okay, Freddie's going to hide in the closet," Carly said.

"And we're going to switch to the Cap Cam in our friend Billy's hat," Sam explained.

"Switching to the Cap Cam," Freddie announced. He wore a mini-control panel on his belt, and now he hit the button for the Cap Cam. Freddie was all the way in the closet now, so the lens in the Cap Cam took over for Freddie's camera.

Sam closed the door on him, and she and Carly dove for their seats.

The lens in Billy's cap picked up all the action as Mr. Howard slammed back into the room.

"I have ears like a hawk!" Mr. Howard yelled. "I distinctly heard laughter, and I hate laughter." He

had no idea he was talking to the entire *iCarly* audience on the Web.

Mr. Howard was entertaining enough all by himself, but he certainly wasn't spectacular.

"Now be quiet!" He pointed at each of them individually to drive his message home. Then he left the room again, slamming the door behind him.

Carly and Sam turned to look into the lens on Billy's cap.

"Isn't he charming?" Carly asked.

"Freddie, let's go," Sam said.

Freddie opened the closet door. "Switching back to main cam," he said, clicking a button on the control panel on his belt. The Cap Cam switched off, and Freddie's camera took over again.

"Okay, we were talking about the things kids do that get them detention," Carly said into Freddie's camera.

Sam walked over to one of the detention students — Rodney. She knew him well. They had detention together a lot. "Why look, here's a gold member of the detention club right here," she said.

"It's ninth-grader Rip Off Rodney," Carly said.

Everyone in school knew Rip Off Rodney. He was always selling something. And it was never worth what he charged for it. Yet somehow, the kids kept on buying.

Rodney stood and waved to the camera. "Please, call me Rip Off," he joked.

"So how'd you get detention?" Carly asked.

"I was selling fake hall passes," Rodney answered proudly.

Fake hall passes. That was something Sam could admire. *"Niiiiiice,"* she said, hitting the applause button on her remote.

"And how'd you get caught?" Carly asked.

Suddenly Rodney was a lot less proud. "I, uh, I misspelled 'hall,'" he said sheepishly.

"Two L's," Carly told him.

Rodney nodded. He knew that — now. "Yeah," he admitted.

"Okay, so have you got anything else to say to the *iCarly* fans of the world?" Sam asked him.

"Yeah," he said. He leaned in close and pointed at the camera. Rip Off Rodney never passed up an opportunity to sell something. "I've got a special

this week on burritos." He opened his jacket. The inside was lined with burritos. "Two for six bucks," he said.

"And do they contain quality meat?" Carly asked the entrepreneur.

"No, they do not," Rodney assured her.

Half the room ran forward, holding out cash.

"I want one!" someone said.

"Over here," Billy said, waving a five-dollar bill.

Carly laughed. It might not be quality meat, but it was definitely a quality *iCarly* moment.

Chapter 6

While everyone else sat at their desks taking a burrito break, Sam and Carly stood in front of a game of hangman they had drawn on the dry erase board. Almost all of the letters were filled in, but no one had guessed the phrase yet. The hangman was still missing two limbs, so there was a chance someone could win the game.

MR _ _WARD EA_S PAN_S

"And now, continuing with our game of hangman . . ." Carly said into the camera.

"J.D., it's your turn to guess a letter or solve the puzzle," Sam told a boy with blond hair sitting in the front row.

J.D. got to his feet and studied the puzzle. "Okay," he said slowly. "Is it 'Mr. Howard eats pants'?" he asked.

"Correct!" Sam said.

"He certainly does!" Carly joked.

Sam pressed her applause button while Carly filled in the remaining letters. J.D. bowed to the camera.

Suddenly, Claire spotted the pants-eater himself. Mr. Howard was heading down the hall. "Dippidy-doo!" she yelled.

"Freddie, hide!" Sam yelled.

"Switching to the Cap Cam!" Freddie said, running for the closet.

The kids ran to their seats and stared into space as if they had been doing that all along. They all did their best to appear miserable.

Seconds later, Mr. Howard burst through the door. "Uh-huh," he said, taking in their clueless expressions. "Everybody's *so* innocent," he said sarcastically. Then he sniffed. "Do I smell burritos?"

No one responded. Rip Off Rodney slowly pulled his jacket closed.

Mr. Howard looked around suspiciously. "I have a feeling," he said, scanning the room. Then he saw the words on the white board and turned back

around very slowly. Steam practically boiled out of his ears. "Who wrote this?" he demanded, pointing at the phrase under the hangman. "Who wrote this lie? Never in my entire life have I eaten one pair of pants!"

He waited for one of the kids to speak up. No one said a word.

"Is someone going to confess? Or do you all want to do two hundred push-ups?" he asked.

Sam raised her hand. She knew the rules of detention better than anyone and Mr. Howard was about to break them. She couldn't allow that. Besides, she hated push-ups. "Principal Franklin says teachers can't give physical punishments in detention," she said.

"Oh, Principal Franklin," Mr. Howard said dismissively. "If you ask me, he's not even fit to be in charge of this school. He's weak. Spineless." Mr. Howard sat on his desk, still completely unaware that he was being filmed, not to mention broadcast over the Web.

"Well, I'm just going to sit right here and stare at you children until detention is over," he said. He picked up the latest edition of *Geometry Now*

magazine and started flipping through it. "And I think I'll add an extra two hours," he said spitefully.

Carly and Sam eyed each other. If all Mr. Howard did was read a magazine, *iCarly*'s fiftieth Web show would turn out to be anything but spectacular. It would be their most boring show ever. It was a good thing they had a backup plan, just in case.

Carly turned around and whispered into the Cap Cam. "Just hang on, Freddie has a way to get rid of Mr. Howard."

Mr. Howard didn't hear Carly, but he did see her whispering to Billy's forehead. "No talking to that boy's hat!" he yelled.

Carly faced front — and fast! She didn't want Mr. Howard to get suspicious.

Meanwhile, Freddie was watching the exchange on his laptop. He dialed his cell phone. "Wesley. Now," he whispered.

Wesley was ready and waiting in the first floor hall. "Check," he said. Wesley wore a headset with

a microphone and had an amplifier on his hip. He turned up the amp and did a quick test, beatboxing into the microphone. It worked.

Next he pulled a brown paper bag with eyeholes over his head, picked up a pot and a ladle, and started beatboxing into the microphone. At the same time, he clanged the pot and the ladle together as loudly as he could — which was really, *really* loudly.

Mr. Howard heard the clanging and the sputtering all the way up on the second floor. It was so loud he couldn't focus on the article he was reading about isosceles triangles. "What in tarnation!" he yelled, walking to the door. He pointed at the class. "Stay here and say nothing."

Sam and Carly jumped to their feet. Sam opened the closet to let Freddie out.

"Switching back to the main cam," Freddie said.

Claire took her lookout position at the door.

"Okay, now that dippidy-doo done gone . . ." Carly said.

". . . next on *iCarly*, live from detention," Sam added.

The girls each held a turtle in front of Freddie's camera. "Turtle races!" they sang together.

Carly thought the turtles were totally adorable, especially hers. "Come on, kiss him," Carly said, holding her turtle right up to the lens.

"Mine wants a big kiss, kiss him," Sam joked.

Out in the hall, Wesley was still beatboxing and banging on his pot. Mr. Howard spotted him from the top of the stairs.

"Hey! You there!" Mr. Howard said, hurrying down the stairs.

Wesley started to run. He couldn't see very well through his paper bag mask, but he ran anyway.

"Stop! Who are you?" Mr. Howard demanded.

Wesley kept running, then he hit a wall.

"Stop, you hooligan!" the teacher yelled.

Wesley wheeled around, ready to run in the other direction, but Mr. Howard was right in front of him.

The teacher had cornered Wesley in front of a wall of lockers. "Remove your sack!" the teacher ordered.

Trapped, Wesley resorted to Plan B. He pulled a water balloon from inside the pot and hurled it at Mr. Howard. It hit the teacher in the chest and splattered. Mr. Howard was soaking wet!

The teacher was too stunned and angry to even say real words. *"Yaaaaggghh!"* he screamed.

Wesley was able to escape, beatboxing as he ran right out of the school.

Mr. Howard could only watch him go, completely bewildered.

He was still staring at the door when Wesley popped his bag-covered head back in the door for a second. "Aye! Aye! Aye!" Wesley screamed.

Meanwhile, in the classroom, the *iCarly* Webcast continued. The turtles were making their extremely slow way to the finish line while kids stood around eating Rip Off Rodney's burritos and cheering on their favorite turtle.

Claire couldn't stand not being in on the action. It sounded like too much fun. She left her post at the door for a second to see what was happening.

"Look at them go!" Sam said into the camera.

"Who says slow can't be exciting?" Carly added.

"You can only get this stuff at iCarly-dot-com, baby!" Sam said to their viewers.

Claire had picked the wrong second to leave her post.

Mr. Howard burst into the room, wet and furious. He caught the kids breaking his rules. "Ha!" he yelled.

Carly's eyes widened. Freddie gulped. Everyone else just froze. They were in trouble now — *big* trouble.

Chapter 7

Carly cringed while Mr. Howard looked around the detention room.

"A video camera! Turtles! Burritos! What is going on in here?" he demanded.

"The *iCarly* Fiftieth Web Show Spectacular," Carly said in a small voice.

Sam hit a button on her remote, filling the room with the sound of cheers and applause.

Carly grabbed the remote from her with a glare. Now wasn't the time!

Mr. Howard's face was bright red. "You're all in real trouble now," he warned them. "I'm talking suspension. Expulsion. Deportation!"

Deportation? Wasn't that a little extreme? Sam wanted to raise her hand and say so, but even she was a little intimidated by the extent of the teacher's anger. Then she saw Principal Franklin quietly

enter the room and stand behind Mr. Howard. Sam relaxed a little bit. Principal Franklin could usually be counted on to be reasonable — for a school official anyway.

Mr. Howard didn't see him. "And you can all start by doing five hundred push-ups, and I don't care what Principal Franklin has to say about it!"

"You don't?" Principal Franklin asked.

"No!" Mr. Howard insisted. Then he realized who had asked the question. "Oh, dear!" Mr. Howard said, spinning around. "Uh, Principal Franklin . . ."

"What are you doing here?" Carly asked the principal.

"Well, I was home watching the *iCarly* Fiftieth Web Show Spectacular," he explained. "Congratulations, by the way. My kids and I love your show."

"Wow," Carly said. She couldn't believe the school principal actually watched their show.

"Awesome," Sam said.

"Thanks," Freddie added.

"And while I was watching, I heard Mr. Howard here call me a weak, spineless fool," the principal continued.

Mr. Howard scrambled to save himself. His tone had changed from angry to nervous. "No, no . . . I said you were sweet, stylish, cool," he stammered.

"In my office," Principal Franklin said firmly.

"But I . . . I . . . I —" Mr. Howard sputtered.

"Now," the principal ordered.

Mr. Howard headed out the door, muttering. "Why does everything always happen to me?"

The kids tried not to laugh too hard at Mr. Howard's predicament. But it was pretty funny. It was the best detention ever!

Sam wondered if the principal would punish them for doing *iCarly* during detention. "So now what?" Sam asked him.

"Well, I suppose Mr. Howard has tortured you all enough," Principal Franklin said to the group. "Go home."

Everyone cheered and ran out of the room — everyone except for Carly, Sam, and Freddie.

Freddie turned his camera on Carly and Sam. It was time to bring the show to a close.

"Okay, we're just about done," Carly said into the camera.

Sam jumped in front of the lens. "I'm Sam."

Carly joined her. "I'm Carly."

Principal Franklin couldn't resist. He leaned into the shot, putting his head between theirs. "And I'm Ted."

Carly laughed. "And thanks for watching *iCarly*'s Fiftieth Web Show Spectacular."

Sam held up the remote, ready to add the closing sound effects.

"May I?" Principal Franklin asked.

Sam handed him the remote. "Second button from the bottom."

Principal Franklin pushed the button and the sound of the Jingle Singers filled the room. "It's *iCarly*'s Fiftieth Web Show Spectacular!" The words flashed across the screen at the same time.

Sam waved good-bye. "Bye! Don't forget to go to iCarly-dot-com."

"See you. Bye!" Carly said, waving too.

"Bye," the principal added.

Freddie counted down the seconds. "And we're clear!" he said, putting down his camera.

Carly, Sam, and Freddie couldn't think of a better way to celebrate their fiftieth Webcast success than by having a pool party. They didn't have a pool, but they had the next best thing — a giant coffee cup filled with decaf coffee.

They went to Carly's loft, put on their bathing suits, and joined Spencer in his coffee cup. It was big enough for all of them.

Sam was cracking up. "How fun is this?"

"It's like a java-cuzzi!" Carly laughed.

"Who wants more coffee?" Spencer asked.

"I do!" they all said.

Carly, Sam, Freddie, and Spencer all raised normal-sized coffee mugs.

They dipped their mugs into the coffee and clinked them together in a toast before taking sips.

"This isn't weird at all!" Carly joked.

Whew! Carly thought. They had not only pulled off *iCarly* from detention, but their fiftieth Web show was truly spectacular — just like they had promised! She couldn't have done it without her best friends, who truly were spectacular.

Read more adventures featuring Carly, Sam, and Freddie!